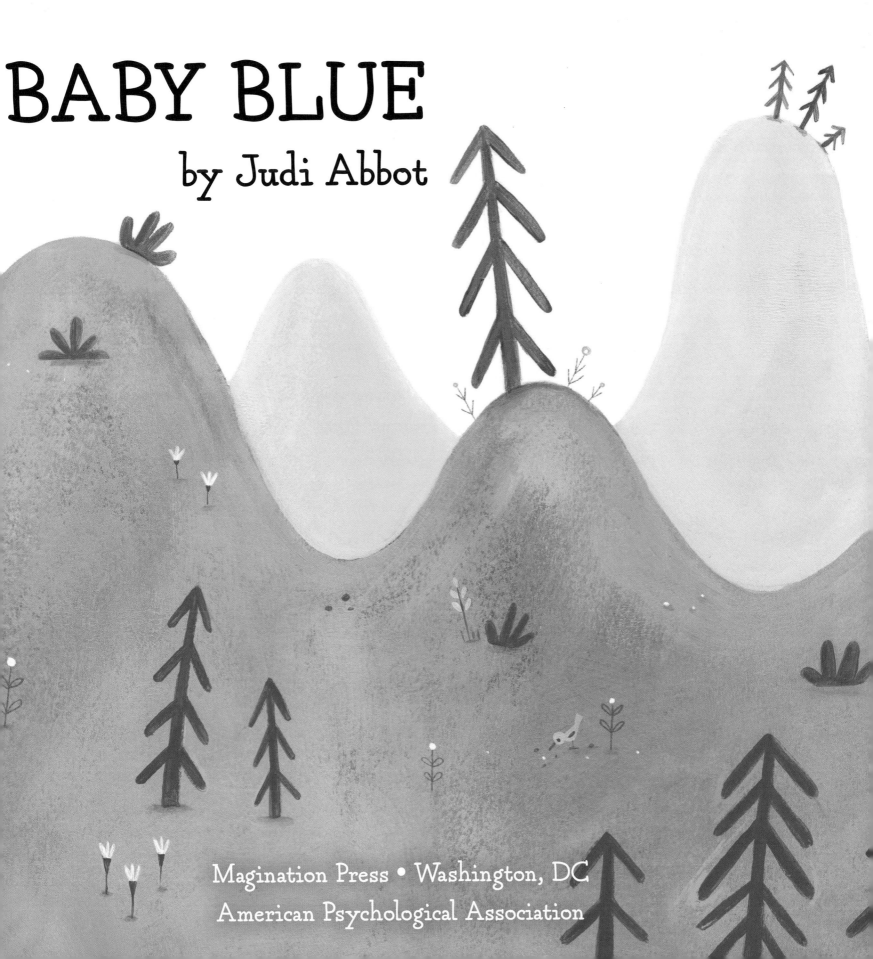

BABY BLUE

by Judi Abbot

Magination Press • Washington, DC
American Psychological Association

There is a book that has a special place in my
heart. *Baby Blue* is a humble tribute to the strong
messages and the simple beauty of
Little Blue and Little Yellow by L. Lionni.

A big thank you to him and to all the people who
helped me in this long creation journey.
And to all the Baby Blue, Yellow, Pink, Purple,
Red, Orange, Green...
—JA

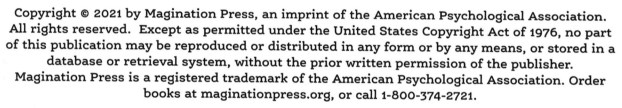

Magination Press

Books for Kids From the
American Psychological Association

maginationpress.org

Book design by Rachel Ross
Printed by Phoenix Color, Hagerstown, MD

Library of Congress Cataloging-in-Publication Data

Names: Abbot, Judi, author, illustrator.
Title: Baby Blue/Judi Abbot.
Description: Washington, DC: Magination Press, [2021] | "American Psychological Association."
| Summary: When a bicycle accident reveals a warm, yellow world beyond his beautiful blue
world, Baby Blue must overcome his fear to reach out to Baby Yellow.
Identifiers: LCCN 2020026595 (print) | LCCN 2020026596 (ebook) | ISBN 9781433833908
(hardcover) | ISBN 9781433834738 (ebook)
Subjects: CYAC: Fear—Fiction. | Friendship—Fiction. | Color—Fiction.
Classification: LCC PZ7.1.A1618 Bab 2021 (print) | LCC PZ7.1.A1618 (ebook) | DDC [E]—dc23
LC record available at https://lccn.loc.gov/2020026595
LC ebook record available at https://lccn.loc.gov/2020026596

Manufactured in the United States of America
10 9 8 7 6 5 4 3 2 1

This is Baby Blue.

Baby Blue lived by himself in a beautiful, blue world

surrounded by beautiful blue trees, flowers, and birds.

When Baby Blue was tired, the dark,
blue Night gently cuddled him to sleep.

"Goodnight, Baby Blue,"
Night whispered.

"Goodnight, Night,"
Baby Blue replied.

One day Baby Blue was racing the blue birds on his bike.

But he didn't notice a big, blue stone on the ground.

Baby Blue checked himself over. He had some little scratches here and there, but he was okay. His bike was fine too...

but something wasn't quite right.

His bike had ripped a hole in his blue world, and a strange, warm light was shining through!

Baby Blue felt a little scared. He had never seen anything so strange before!

"I'm going to be brave," he whispered to himself, and peered through the hole.

In front of him there was a whole new world! Everything was that same warm color: the trees, the birds, the flowers, and... someone else.

Someone strange!

Suddenly he stopped pedaling
and stared right at Baby Blue.

"Oh no, he saw me!"
Baby Blue thought, and
he jumped on his blue
bike and pedaled away
as fast as he could.

He finally stopped under the shade of a big, blue tree to catch his breath. His mind was so full of questions!

When Night came again, Baby Blue felt a little braver. He looked again through the hole at the warm and welcoming light of the new world.

He did it again the next night, and the night after that. Soon, the other side did not look so different or so scary.

Finally Baby Blue decided it was time. He took a bright, blue stone from the ground and he drew a little smiling face on it.

You are my magic stone,

he said.

With you in my pocket, I'm not going to be scared of anything!

He took a big, deep breath, and climbed through the hole.

Hello!

Nice to meet you!
I'm Baby Yellow.

I was waiting for you!

I hope your bike isn't broken.

I can drive it with one hand, can you?

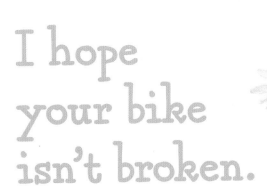

Do you want to see my bike?

I'm very fast.

Baby Blue was so happy and relieved that he didn't know what to say, so he reached into his pocket and gave Baby Yellow his bright, blue, smiling stone with a gentle, "Hello!"

Baby Blue and Baby Yellow played together that whole day, and the day after that, and every day to follow. Pretty soon they became best friends.

They raced together
through Baby Blue's cool,
blue world on their bikes.

They laughed and played and sang
in Baby Yellow's bright yellow world.

The more time they spent together,
the more things started to change...

...and a beautiful new color began to appear!

What other
new worlds
might be
waiting for them?